Little Jack Rabbit And The *Squirrel Brothers*

David Cory

LITTLE JACK RABBIT AND THE SQUIRREL BROTHERS
THE GAME OF MARBLES

Never stop upon your way,

Just to fool around and play.

Learn to quickly go to school;

Never, never break this rule.

BUT, oh dear me. One morning when Little Jack Rabbit met the Squirrel Brothers, Featherhead, the naughty gray squirrel, asked him to stop and play a game of marbles.

"Where are your marbles?" asked the little rabbit.

"Here they are," answered Featherhead, taking some red and yellow oak apples out of his pocket. "They make dandy marbles."

Little Jack Rabbit dropped his school books, and quickly dug a hole in the ground. Then they all took turns rolling the marbles to see who would have the first shot.

The little bunny's was the first to drop into the hole, although Twinkle Tail's was very close and Featherhead's not far away.

It was then easy for Little Jack Rabbit to hit the two marbles. Why, he couldn't miss them, they were so close. I guess they would have been playing until now if all of a sudden, just like that, Bobbie Redvest hadn't called out:

"Ding-a-ling! ding-a-ling! the school bell is ringing."

"Gracious me!" cried little bunny, and off he went, clipperty clip, lipperty lip. Featherhead and Twinkle Tail picked up their books and followed.

It certainly was lucky that the little robin had shouted, "Ding-a-ling! ding-a-ling!" for hardly had they reached the top of the hill when the school bell commenced: "Ding, dong! ding, dong! ding, dong!"

"Hurry up!" cried Little Jack Rabbit, "or we'll be late," and he hopped along faster than ever.

Professor Crow was standing in the doorway waiting for the last scholar to arrive.

All out of breath and scared to death,

Came little Jackie Bunny.

And Twinkle Tail began to quail,

And Featherhead felt funny.

They thought the teacher standing there

Gave them a cold and angry stare.

Perhaps he did, but soon he went

And o'er his platform table bent,

While Featherhead and Twinkle Tail

Slipped in their seats with faces pale.

Then up stood stern Professor Crow

And said some scholars are so slow

That if they'd stop upon the way

They'd never get to school all day.

Then he sat down and called the school to order. But, oh dear me! None of the little marble players knew his lesson. And instead of being allowed to go when school was over, they were kept in and made to study until late in the afternoon.

A LITTLE PIECE OF LOOKING GLASS

If you a naughty act will do,
You may at first escape;
But soon or later you'll get caught—
So don't get in a scrape.

FEATHERHEAD was the worst pupil in the Shady Forest School and made lots of trouble for Professor Crow.

One day he held a small piece of looking glass in the sunlight. The flash almost blinded the poor old crow's eyes, and at first he couldn't tell who had done it. But naughtiness will always out, and the next time Featherhead was caught.

Yes, sir! The next time he tried it on Professor Crow, that old gentleman bird jumped down from the platform and took hold of that naughty squirrel's ear. And not so very gently, either.

Featherhead squirmed and tried to get away, but the good professor held on tight, and pretty soon the little squirrel grew very quiet indeed. He grew as quiet as a little lamb; that's what he did.

"Young man!" said Professor Crow in a hard, stern voice, "your father, Squirrel Nutcracker, is a dear old friend of mine. If it weren't for that I'd give you a flogging."

Goodness me! When Featherhead heard that he trembled all over, and his beautiful bushy tail lost its curl and dragged on the floor like a piece of string!

"You're a bad lot," went on the old professor bird. "You never know your lessons, and if you don't mend your ways I'll expel you from the school!"

Gracious me! Think of having that said to you! Goosey Lucy's little son, Goosey Gander, almost fell off the dunce stool, and Little Jack Rabbit was so frightened that his little pink nose trembled for an hour.

Nobody played games during recess that day, but hung around in little groups talking it over. And you may be sure they kept away from Featherhead, who stood all alone by the flag pole wishing he hadn't been such a bad squirrel.

THE FLEET

SOMETHING had happened in the Shady Forest since Busy Beaver had built his dam. You see, as it held back the Bubbling Brook, the water grew deeper and deeper, and by and by it began to spread all around, until after a while, there was a pond.

This didn't trouble the Little People of the Shady Forest. No, indeed. They liked to have a pond in the forest. But they didn't like to have the Big Chestnut Tree right in the middle of it. No, sir. The water had spread all around the biggest and finest nut tree in the whole forest, and, of course, now no one could gather the nuts.

"What are we going to do?" asked Chippy Chipmunk.

"Make a boat and sail over," answered Featherhead, the gray squirrel. This wasn't a bad idea, but who was going to make the boat? Nobody in the Shady Forest knew how to build one.

Professor Crow suggested that the birds carry the nuts for the four-footed people, but they answered that they had all they could do to feed themselves and couldn't spare the time. And Grandmother Magpie said she wouldn't carry nuts for anybody, even if she had all the time that was wasted every day by some people right there in the Shady Forest.

Just then along came Old Squirrel Nutcracker.

"Why not make rafts out of twigs? You don't need a boat builder for that, you know."

This seemed a splendid idea, and at once all the squirrels set to work, and in a short time quite a fleet was ready to be launched. There wasn't room for more than one squirrel on a raft, so some of the squirrels had to stay ashore.

Featherhead was the first to shove off. He had a little sack and a large oar, and spread out his tail for a sail.

Billy Breeze was very kind and blew the rafts over to the island on which the Big Chestnut Tree stood. Then all the squirrels went ashore and commenced to fill their sacks with nuts, when, all of a sudden, Old Barney Owl looked out of his nest and said:

"This is my tree and these nuts belong to me. If you wish any, you must pay a penny!"

"If we bring you something to-morrow, will that do?" asked Twinkle Tail.

"Yes," answered the old owl.

So the squirrels filled their sacks and sailed home.

But soon the news from Squirrelville

Spread o'er the meadow to the hill,

And up the Shady Forest Trail,

And through the quiet verdant vale.

It's strange how Rumor quickly goes;

It runs on very nimble toes,

And everybody hears the news

Before it has worn out its shoes.

MORE NUTS

IT wasn't very long before all the Little People in the Shady Forest had heard how the squirrels had sailed over to the island after nuts. So when Featherhead and the other squirrels set out the next day there was quite a crowd on shore to watch them.

Featherhead had a nice new-laid egg from Henny Penny for Old Barney Owl, and Twinkle Tail a little fish from the Bubbling Brook.

When they reached the island, the two little squirrels ran up the Big Chestnut Tree and rapped on Old Barney Owl's front door. They had to rap three or four times before he opened it. He was cross and sleepy, and at first didn't remember them at all. Infact, his eyes were so blinky that I don't believe he even saw them.

"We have brought you an egg for the nuts we took yesterday," said Featherhead.

"And here is a little fish for what we'll take to-day," added Twinkle Tail.

Old Barney Owl opened one eye and, taking the egg and the little fish, closed the door without even thanking them.

"He didn't say we could have any nuts to-day," said Twinkle Tail. "He took the little fish, so I guess it's all right."

"Guess it's all right!" cried Featherhead. "Of course, it's all right. What do we care, anyway? he can't see in the light. What right has Old Barney to say all these nuts belong to him?"

It didn't take the squirrels long after the sacks were filled to carry them down to the shore and load them on the rafts. But, oh dear me. Billy Breeze wasn't very kind this time. No matter how they held up their tails for sails, as soon as they had pushed off, he blew them right back on the land.

"We'll have to paddle around to the other side," said Featherhead. "Then perhaps Billy Breeze will push us home."

After a good deal of trouble, for it was no easy matter to paddle the rafts around the island, they set off once again. And this time Billy Breeze did his best, and landed them safely on the mainland.

"I couldn't help you on the other side," he explained. "You see, I can blow only one way to-day."

"That's all right," answered the Squirrel Brothers. "We have the nuts!" and away they scampered.

OLD SQUIRREL NUTCRACKER

TWINKLE TAIL and Featherhead were old enough to find homes for themselves, so Old Squirrel Nutcracker thought. And when that old squirrel had thought out a thing seriously he was pretty likely to put it into words.

"I feel sorry for the boys," said Mrs. Nutcracker, wiping her eyes with her calico apron, as she stood beneath the Big Chestnut Tree talking to Mrs. Rabbit. "They've had such a comfortable home, if I do say it myself. But last night Squirrel Nutcracker said after dinner:

"'Boys, it's time for you to get out and hustle for yourselves. It will make men-squirrels out of you. If you get into trouble, always remember your father will help you. And don't forget your mother.'"

Poor Mrs. Nutcracker threw her apron over her head and burst into tears. "Don't cry," said the kind bunny lady, and very soon she said good-by and hopped home to the Old Bramble Patch to tell her little rabbit the news.

When Mrs. Nutcracker reached home she found her little squirrel boys packing up their things. Twinkle Tail had his nearly finished, but Featherhead was only half through. So Mrs. Nutcracker helped him, and when it was all done, she sat down and cried again. Poor Mrs. Nutcracker felt so badly she just couldn't help it.

Just then Old Squirrel Nutcracker came up the stairs, so she dried her eyes and the two little squirrels picked up their trunks and started down the tree.

When they reached the first landing, a great big limb that spread out to one side, there stood Squirrel Nutcracker. His voice was a little husky as he said:

"I want to be proud of you, Twinkle Tail and Featherhead. See that you find nice homes and that you don't do anything to make me ashamed of you." Then he hugged them good-by and went upstairs to Mrs. Nutcracker.

HOME HUNTING

IT was a week or so after the Squirrel Brothers had left Nutcracker Lodge to find homes for themselves that Little Jack Rabbit came across Twinkle Tail.

It's not an easy thing to find a new home, especially when all the nice warm hollow trees were already crowded with little people. Twinkle Tail discovered this when he started in house-hunting.

"Why don't you take Grandmother Magpie's nest?" asked the little rabbit. "She hasn't used it for some time and nobody seems to want it." This was very true; perhaps it was because nobody liked Grandmother Magpie.

But after Twinkle Tail had taken it over you never would have known it. You see, he altered it and arranged it and patched it up to suit himself.

While he was putting on the finishing touches, who should come along but the old lady magpie herself.

"Do you mind my doing this to your old place?" he asked, looking up from his work.

"Not at all," replied Grandmother Magpie, "I'm done with it. You're quite welcome to it, my dear."

This was the first time she had ever done a nice thing for anybody in the Shady Forest. But, you see, she liked Twinkle Tail. He was the only person she did like. I guess the reason was that she had never forgotten he had once been very polite to her.

"Thank you," said Twinkle Tail, smiling sweetly, and then he set to work harder than ever.

After that the old lady magpie flew away, thinking how strange it was that a house which one has grown tired of often suits another person very well.

By and by Twinkle Tail had another caller. It was Bobbie Redvest.

"How do you like the way I'm fixing up my house?" asked the little squirrel.

"I think you've made one mistake," replied Bobbie Redvest.

"What is it?" asked Twinkle Tail anxiously.

"The great thing, you know, is to hide your house as much as possible."

The little squirrel dropped the piece of green moss he was about to use, and waited.

"You should make it look like the place it's in," went on the little robin. "You have chosen a browny place, so you must use brown moss on the outside."

"That sounds like good advice," said Twinkle Tail. "I'll do as you say."

Here a leaf and there a twig,

Piece of twine to bind them —

Then some moss to spread across,

Till it's hard to find them.

Soon the tiny Treetop House

Will be built and ready;

Dry beneath the pelting rain,

Against the wind quite steady.

AN OLD CROW'S NEST

NOW Featherhead had a much harder time finding a home than Brother Twinkle Tail. He traveled from the oaks to the beech trees, jumping from branch to branch, peeping first into this place and then into that, but every hole and hollow had a tenant.

By and by he ran down to the ground and along the winding paths through the leaves and brush, but even then he could find nothing. No, sir. There didn't seem to be a single place in the whole big forest for this little squirrel.

"Goodness me!" he exclaimed, "what shall I do? I don't want to go back to Nutcracker Lodge and tell them I can't look out for myself. I'd feel like a baby." So he sat down to think it over.

All of a sudden who should come by but Jimmy Crow.

"What's the matter? You look dreadfully worried."

"And so I am," replied the little squirrel. "And so would you be if you couldn't find a home for yourself."

Jimmy Crow turned his head first to one side and then to the other, and winked his bright little eye. Then he winked the other several times. After that he wagged his feathered tail and opened both eyes.

"I know just the place for you."

"You don't mean it," cried Featherhead.

"I certainly do," replied Jimmy Crow, "if you'll follow me I'll take you there in a jiffy." And Jimmie Crow knew what he was about, for he quickly led the little squirrel to a tall oak tree whose acorns lay in heaps all over the ground. Way up high on a branch was an old crow's nest.

"There's the place for you," cried Jimmy Crow. "You can fix it up in no time."

Featherhead thanked him and ran up the tree to look it over. It didn't take him long to make up his mind what to do. Pressing the sticks more closely together, he covered them overhead and all around with leafy twigs, until it looked like a great big ball of leaves. In one side he made a little round hole for a doorway, and as the roof was nicely rounded, and this was the only opening, the rain couldn't get inside.

"With a good supply of nuts," he laughed, "I won't have to go down to the ground for my meals, and can sleep for days at a time when it's cold and stormy!"

My little house up in the tree

Is just the very thing for me.

It holds my food and keeps the rain

From off my comfy counterpane.

But sometimes it seems lonely quite

When fall the shadows of the night,

And I have no one but myself

To climb up to the pantry shelf.

PARSON OWL EXPLAINS

ONE day as Twinkle Tail was taking a walk through the treetops, he met a young lady squirrel. She was anxiously looking here and there as if in search of something.

"Are you looking for anybody?" asked Twinkle Tail, lifting his little fur cap and bowing politely.

"Not exactly," she replied, "I'm looking for a furnished apartment. Do you know of one?"

Twinkle Tail didn't answer at once. He wanted to say something, but as he was a bashful little squirrel, it took him some time to make up his mind. Miss Squirrel, however, was not the least impatient, but curled her beautiful bushy tail up over her back and looked her prettiest.

At last he said: "Why don't you share my house? It's a very nice sort of a place since I fixed it up. It once belonged to Grandmother Magpie, you know."

After little Miss Squirrel had looked it over, she seemed greatly pleased, especially with the kitchenette, in which were stored lots of beech nuts, hazels and fir-cones. And I think she was even more pleased with Twinkle Tail, for she agreed to get married to him at once. So off he started for Parson Owl and a little gold ring, while she went into the kitchenette to get the wedding supper.

On his way he met little Jack Rabbit.

"I'm going to get married to-day! Come to my house this afternoon at five," shouted Twinkle Tail.

"All right," answered the little rabbit. "I'll run home to tell mother."

Pretty soon Twinkle Tail met Squirrel Nutcracker.

"I knew there was going to be a wedding," he exclaimed, when he heard the news. "I saw three magpies this very morning, and that's a sure sign." Then he patted the little squirrel's head and promised that he and Mrs. Nutcracker would surely come.

By the time Twinkle Tail reached the parsonage at the top of the old oak tree it was quite late. "Have you got the wedding ring?" asked Parson Owl as the little squirrel turned to go.

"Goodness gracious meebus!" exclaimed Twinkle Tail, "I've forgotten all about it."

Parson Owl yawned, for it's only in the night-time that owls are wide awake, you know, and replied:

"Can't marry you without a ring. No, indeed. Who ever heard of a wedding without a ring?"

(Parson Owl was wide awake enough to know that! Goodness me! I hope the little squirrel will find a jewelry store somewhere in the Shady Forest.)

THE LITTLE GOLD RING

TWINKLE TAIL felt dreadfully worried as he left the parsonage. Where was he to get the ring? Without it, Parson Owl had said there could be no wedding. Little Miss Squirrel was waiting for him at the house, and all the guests would be there at five o'clock. Parson Owl had agreed to be on time although it was a trifle too bright at that hour for his blinky old eyes. There was only one thing missing — the little gold wedding ring.

"There's only one person who can help me," cried Twinkle Tail, and off he ran to the Old Bramble Patch. In answer to hisimpatient knock, Little Jack Rabbit opened the door. Then they both sat down on the stone step while the little squirrel told his troubles one by one.

"Parson Owl says there can't be a wedding without a ring," sighed Twinkle Tail, finishing his story. "But where to get the ring, I don't know."

"I do," answered the little rabbit, jumping up quickly. "Come with me," and up the Old Cow Patch, over the Sunny Meadow, he hopped with Twinkle Tail close to his heels.

By and by they came to the Old Farm Yard. There stood Ducky Waddles by the old creaking gate. He had just come in from a swim in the Old Duck Pond and was combing his feathers with his big yellow bill.

"Good afternoon," said the little bunny. "I've come to ask a favor."

"What is it?" asked Ducky Waddles.

"You explain matters first, Twinkle Tail, and then I'll talk to Ducky Waddles," said Little Jack Rabbit.

It didn't take Twinkle Tail long to tell his troubles — how little Miss Squirrel had agreed to marry him that afternoon; how all the little people of the Shady Forest were coming to the wedding at five; how Parson Owl had agreed to marry them; how everything was ready except the little gold wedding ring.

"Who told you I had a little gold ring?" asked Ducky Waddles.

"Nobody," answered the little squirrel, "but I suppose it's all right."

"Yes, it's all right," laughed Ducky Waddles with a funny quack, "and now, Mr. Jack Rabbit, what's the favor you wish me to do?"

"Won't you give Twinkle Tail the little gold ring you found in the Bubbling Brook last Sunday?"

Ducky Waddles took a little gold ring out of his feather waistcoat pocket and handed it to Twinkle Tail.

(Pretty soon we'll hear the wedding bells tinkling in the forest dells.)

WEDDING BELLS

TWINKLE TAIL was delighted to get the little gold ring.

"You must come to the wedding," he said to Ducky Waddles. "It's to be at five o'clock at my house. Please tell Henny Penny and Cocky Doodle that they're invited, and ask Goosey Lucy and Turkey Tim to come, too. I'm in such a hurry I can't wait to see them."

"I'll come," answered Ducky Waddles, "and I won't forget to tell the Barnyard Folk that they're invited."

"Don't lose the ring," cautioned Little Jack Rabbit, as he and the little squirrel hurried down the Old Cow Path to the Shady Forest. Just then they met Mrs. Cow. She was wagging her head back and forth to brush off the flies and the little bell on her leather collar made a pretty tinkling sound.

"Let's ask her to come and ring the wedding bells."

"The very thing," laughed Twinkle Tail. "Won't you come to my wedding, Mrs. Cow? Please do."

"When is it to be?" she asked.

"To-night at five," answered Twinkle Tail, with a blush.

"Pretty near milking-time," explained Mrs. Cow.

"Oh, it won't take long," replied the little rabbit. "Do come, Mrs. Cow. We want you to ring your bell at the wedding. Did you ever ring a wedding bell?"

"No," answered Mrs. Cow, "but I guess I know how. I'll come, but I may not be able to stay all the time for I must get back in time for milking."

Then the three started off together, and when they reached the Shady Forest, Twinkle Tail looked back and saw Henny Penny and Cocky Doodle coming up the Old Cow Path dressed in their Sunday clothes. Just behind them were Ducky Waddles and Goosey Lucy and in the distance Turkey Tim hurrying along the Old Rail Fence to catch up to them.

"Goodness me!" exclaimed the little squirrel, "I won't have much time to dress," and he set off at a great pace, leaving Mrs. Cow and Little Jack Rabbit behind.

When he reached his house he found Miss Squirrel anxiously looking out of the window, but when she saw him, she laughed and said, "I thought you were lost, dear Twinkle Tail!"

Pretty soon Parson Owl arrived, and when all the guests were seated, he told Twinkle Tail and Miss Squirrel to stand up before him. And after Twinkle Tail had placed the little gold ring on Miss Squirrel's little finger toe, Mrs. Cow rang the wedding bells and Bobbie Redvest sang a song.

"NUTS AND RAISINS"

THERE was a grand feast after the wedding of Twinkle Tail and little Miss Squirrel. There were nuts and raisins for everybody, and I don't know of anything much nicer than nuts and raisins.

Of course, all the Barnyard Folk ate raisins, for they couldn't crack the nuts. It almost gave Ducky Waddles a toothache watching Twinkle Tail crack the shells.

Cocky Doodle made a pretty speech, wishing the Twinkle Tails a long life and a happy one, in which all the little people of the forest joined him.

After that everybody looked at the wedding presents, which if not beautiful, were very useful.

Henny Penny gave a nice new laid egg and Turkey Tim a bag of corn. Little Jack Rabbit brought a big carrot and Chippy Chipmunk a basket of nuts. Of course Ducky Waddles didn't give them anything more—the little gold ring was his present, which Twinkle Tail had slipped on the little toe-finger of Miss Squirrel at a nod from Parson Owl.

You see, Twinkle Tail had never been married before, so Parson Owl had helped him a little—which I presume all good kind ministers do when they marry young people. At any rate, Parson Owl did, and so everything went off very smoothly.

On the way home if it hadn't been for some friendly Fireflies, Little Jack Rabbit might have lost his way. And then again, maybe not, for he was a pretty bright little bunny and like all the Forest Folk, knew how to take care of himself. At the same time, it's nice to have a lantern on a dark night. One might, you know, stumble into a deep hole.

When they reached the Old Bramble Patch, the little rabbit said: "I'd ask you in, only I'm afraid mother's asleep."

"Thank you just the same," answered the kind Fireflies. "We are glad to have helped you with our little lanterns," and they flew away to the Sunny Meadow to wink and blink like little stars among the tall grasses.

The little rabbit opened the door and hopped softly up to his room and was soon fast asleep in his comfortable bed.

BAD NEWS

It's really too bad that the Miller's Boy

Should be snooping around with his gun.

Why doesn't he stay in the Old Mill all day

And leave little folks to their fun?

THAT'S what the Little People of the Shady Forest and the Sunny Meadow thought. You see, the Miller's Boy had very little to do just now, for the farmers were busy in the fields and the corn wasn't ready to be ground into meal. So all the Miller's Boy had to do was to attend to a few chores and then get out his gun and go hunting. And of course all the little four-footed and feathered people were dreadfully afraid of that great noisy gun.

"Look here," said Mrs. Rabbit, one day to her little son, "you had better be careful. You can't run faster than a bullet, you know. It's all very well to run away from Danny Fox and Mr. Wicked Weasel, or to dodge from under Hungry Hawk, but a bullet is a different thing," and the kind lady bunny patted her small son on the left ear and gave him a piece of cherry pie.

Well, as soon as the pie was gone, Little Jack Rabbit hopped out of the Old Bramble Patch, clipperty clip, lipperty lip, and pretty soon he met Chippy Chipmunk and Woody Chuck in the Shady Forest.

"Mother says a bullet goes faster than Danny Fox," explained the little bunny, and as everybody in the Shady Forest knew Mrs. Rabbit never told anything that wasn't true, as Grandmother Magpie did, for instance, these two little friends looked very serious. Yes, indeed, they looked serious. They began to feel that the Miller's Boy was a dangerous person.

"Let's tell all our friends," said Woody Chuck, so off the three started and by and by, not so very far, they came to the Shady Forest Pond where Busy Beaver lived.

"Pooh, pooh!" he said, when he heard the news. "I'm safe in the water. He can't get a shot at me."

"Don't be too sure," answered Little Jack Rabbit, as he ran down to the Old Duck Pond to tell Granddaddy "

Now the old gentleman frog was half asleep on his log, his chin resting on his gray waistcoat and his eyes closed, for he had just eaten a big dinner of flies.

"Helloa, there, Granddaddy Bullfrog," shouted the little rabbit. The old frog opened his eyes and took out his watch to see the time, for he thought at first it was Mrs. Bullfrog calling him home.

"Oh, it's you, is it?" he said to the little rabbit. "Gracious me, I must have fallen asleep, for I had a dream.

"I thought I'd caught a thousand flies,

All on this summer day.

But now that you've awakened me

They all have flown away.

"Oh, it was such a pleasant dream,

I fear I shall grow thinner.

You should have let me slumber on

Until I'd finished dinner."

POOR JIMMY MINK

AS soon as Little Rabbit had told the old gentleman frog to watch out for the Miller's Boy, he hopped along by the Bubbling Brook, as it wound in and out among the trees of the Shady Forest or went splashing over rocks and fallen logs. All of a sudden he met Jimmy Mink. But, oh dear me! What was the matter with Jimmy Mink? He was hobbling on three legs. What could be the matter?

"Helloa, there, Jimmy Mink," shouted the little rabbit.

"What makes you walk on three legs,

When you can walk on four?

I didn't know that you had been

A soldier in the war."

"I haven't," replied Jimmy Mink. "I got caught in a trap," and he lifted up his right foreleg.

"Why, your foot's gone!" gasped the little rabbit. "Isn't that dreadful?"

"Yes, it's pretty bad," answered Jimmy Mink. "But the only way I could free myself was to bite off my foot."

"Oh! oh! oh!" cried the little rabbit, sorrowfully. "Tell me how it happened." So Jimmy Mink explained how one day when he had crept out of his little house under the bank of the Bubbling Brook, he had seen a nice fat trout on an old log. "There was a queer looking iron thing there, too," he said, "but I didn't think anything about that. But, oh dear me! When I picked up the trout, something snapped and my leg was caught fast. Oh, how it pinched! I pulled and pulled. But I couldn't get away. Then I tried to bite the iron thing that held my foot, but I couldn't break it. So at last I gnawed off my foot."

"Whew!" whistled the little bunny through his teeth. "I never could do that. My, but you're a brave fellow."

"There's the iron thing over there," said Jimmy Mink, pointing to a trap that lay on an old log close to the bank. The little rabbit hopped over and looked at it. And, sure enough, pinched in between the jaws of the cruel trap was Jimmy Mink's little black foot.

"But I've learned my lesson," said Jimmy Mink. "Next time if I want trout, I'll catch him in the water, not on top of a log,"and he jumped into the pool and swam away. Then the little rabbit hopped along the Shady Forest Trail, but he couldn't forget poor little Jimmy Mink.

Well, after a while, all of a sudden, he heard a great chickering and chirring overhead. Around and around the trunk of the tree went two bodies, one a yellowish brown, about as large as a cat, and the other gray, with a long bushy tail.

Up to the top they went as fast as lightning, around and around, corkscrew fashion, and then down they came to the ground and before his yellowish brown enemy could catch him, Twinkle Tail dashed into a crack between two stones.

PROFESSOR JIM CROW'S LESSON

"I'M so glad Twinkle Tail got away," said Little Jack Rabbit to himself, as the frightened gray squirrel squeezed in between the rocks. And then the little rabbit hopped away as fast as he could, and pretty soon he saw Professor Jim Crow with his little Black Book in his claw.

"Tell me, Professor Jim Crow," said the little rabbit, "what is the name of the yellowish-brown animal that chases little gray squirrels around and around the trunks of trees?"

"How big was he?" asked the wise old bird, putting on his spectacles and turning over the leaves of his little Black Book.

"Larger than the farmer's black cat," answered the little rabbit.

"Did it look something like a fox?" asked the old crow.

"Yes, he did," replied the little rabbit.

Professor Jim Crow smiled and turned to page 49. "Listen!" he said. "The Marten looks very much like a young fox about two months old. Its color is a yellowish-brown, a little darker than a yellow fox, with a number of long black hairs. It is a great climber, hunts squirrels and robs birds' nests."

Then the wise old crow closed his book and wiped his spectacles. "You have learned something to-day, little rabbit. Mother Nature's School House will teach you lots of things," and the old professor bird flew away.

"Well, I'm going to have a good time now," thought the little rabbit to himself. "I've learned my daily lesson. I'll call up Uncle John." So off he hopped to the Hollow Stump Telephone Booth.

"What number do you want?" asked the telephone girl who was a little wood-mouse.

"One, two, three, Harefield," answered the little rabbit, and in less than five hundred short seconds, he heard his Uncle's voice over the wire.

"Goodness gracious meebus!" exclaimed Mr. John Hare, "I thought you'd forgotten all about your old uncle. Where are you?"

"I'm in the Hollow Stump Telephone Booth," answered the little rabbit.

"I'll come right over to the Old Bramble Patch," said Uncle John, and the old gentleman hare dropped the receiver on his lefthind toe he was so excited. You see, he hadn't heard from his little bunny nephew for so long that he supposed he had enlisted in Uncle Sam's Army or Aunt Columbia's Navy! Well, anyway, as soon as the little rabbit had paid the little wood-mouse five carrot cents, he hopped home to tell his mother that Uncle John Hare was coming over to supper.

TO THE POST OFFICE

" BILLY BREEZE, please blow no more

The leaves around the kitchen door.

It takes my time till ten fifteen

To make the doorstep nice and clean,"

said Little Jack Rabbit the next morning after he had polished the front doorknob and fed the canary and filled the woodbox in the kitchen with kindling wood.

Oh, my, yes, he was a busy little rabbit. He had to help his mother in lots of ways, especially when Uncle John Hare was making a visit at the Old Bramble Patch.

Well, when the little rabbit had done all these things, his mother asked him to go down to the post office and buy her three War Savings Stamps and the Rabbitville Gazette for Uncle John, who had a touch of rheumatism in his left hind toe and didn't feel like hopping around, but preferred to sit in an armchair on the back stoop where it was warm and sunny.

Now, as Little Jack Rabbit hopped along, he met Chippy Chipmunk under the Big Chestnut Tree, so of course he stopped and said good morning.

"Where are you going?" asked the little Chipmunk. And when he found out, he took two twenty-five carrot cent pieces out of his pocket and asked the little rabbit to buy him two Thrift Stamps.

"All right," said the little bunny, dropping the two quarters in his knapsack, and by and by, not so very far, he met Squirrel Nutcracker.

"Where are you going?" asked the old gray squirrel.

"Down to the Post Office," answered the little rabbit.

"Will you buy me a dollar's worth of Thrift Stamps, please," said Squirrel Nutcracker. So the little rabbit tucked the lettuce dollar bill in his waistcoat pocket and hopped along. And pretty soon, not so very far, he met Busy Beaver. He was plastering the top of his little mud house and was dreadfully busy, but when he heard where Little Jack Rabbit was going, he put his little muddy paw in his pocket and took out a fifty cent piece.

"Please buy me two Thrift Stamps, I've no time to go to the village. I must finish my house before the frost comes."

The little rabbit put the fifty cent piece in his knapsack and hopped along, and by and by Parson Owl, who sat winking and blinking in his Hollow Tree House, called out to the little rabbit as he hopped over the dry leaves:

"Hey, there! Where are you going?"

"Down to the Post Office to buy stamps!"

"Will you buy me ten dollars' worth if I give you the money?" asked the winky, blinky old owl. Goodness me; it will take another story to tell what happened after that.

MORE STAMPS

NOW let me see. We left little Billy Bunny on his way to the Post Office to buy Thrift Stamps and the Rabbitville Gazette. And, oh dear me! I'm all mixed up. I can't remember whether Timmy Chipmunk gave the little rabbit ten dollars or whether Old Parson Owl did. Or whether the Squirrel Brothers wanted two stamps, or whether it was Busy Beaver who wanted three, or maybe four and perhaps five. Oh dear me again!

But never mind. I guess the little rabbit wasn't mixed up, for he hopped along as happy as you please, and just before he cameto Rabbitville, he heard a voice in the treetops say:

"Where are you going, little Hoppity Hop,

You're going so fast maybe you can't stop."

"Oh, yes, I can," answered Little Jack Rabbit. "What do you want?"

"That depends on where you are going," said Professor Jim Crow, for it was the old blackbird who had stopped the little rabbit, you see.

"I'm going to the Post Office to buy Mother Three Thrift Stamps and Uncle John the Rabbitville Gazette, and let me see. Oh, yes; oh, yes. Chippy Chipmunk gave me two quarters to buy him two Thrift Stamps, and Squirrel Nutcracker handed me a lettuce dollar bill to buy him four, and Busy Beaver gave me a fifty-cent piece to buy him two, and Parson Owl just now pinned in my inside pocket a ten-dollar lettuce bill to pay for forty stamps."

"I wonder what he wants so many stamps for?" said Professor Jim Crow. "Why doesn't he buy a Liberty Bond?"

"Maybe he wants to give them away," answered the little rabbit. "But I mustn't stop—I must be going."

"Wait, wait," said Professor Jim Crow. "Here's some money. Buy me ten Thrift Stamps," and he handed over a two and one-half dollar lettuce bill. "Don't lose the half," added the wise old crow, and then he flew up into his old pine tree and cawed away right merrily. And after that the little rabbit hopped along and when he came to the Post Office, he went up to the little stamp window and asked the old maid grasshopper, who was the postmistress, you remember—but if you don't, she was, just the same, for Bobbie Redvest told me so—if there were any letters. But there was only the Rabbitville Gazette done up in a pink wrapper and yellow two-cent stamp.

"Have you Thrift Stamps?" asked Bunny Boy. And when the lady grasshopper said yes, he told her just how many he wanted, for he could remember everything, you see, which is more than I can, let me tell you, unless I look back over this story. And after he had put the stamps carefully in his knapsack with little pieces of wax paper between so that they wouldn't stick together, he started back for the Old Bramble Patch. And in the next story, if all those stamps don't get angry and try to lick each other, I'll tell you what happened after that.

BUSY TIMES

WHEN Little Jack Rabbit finally reached home with the stamps and the Rabbitville Gazette, he found his Uncle John singing at the piano this lovely song:

The Autumn leaves are falling

Along the Woodland ways,

In scarlet, brown and yellow coats

These cool November days.

They rustle by the Old Rail Fence,

They whisper in the lane,

Or from the shivering half-clad trees

They sing a sad refrain.

But Mrs. Rabbit was too busy putting up carrot preserves and lettuce pickles to even listen. All the little people of the ShadyForest and Sunny Meadow were getting ready for Winter.

The little feathered people were pruning their wings for a long flight to the warm Southland, and the four-footed folk were gathering nuts and grain for their storehouses.

The Squirrel Brothers had a bushel of nuts, and maybe more, laid away carefully in the old chestnut tree, and Chippy Chipmunk had filled his underground storeroom with nuts and corn.

Granddaddy Bullfrog was almost ready to dive into the Old Duck Pond to hide in the soft warm mud. Teddy Turtle, too, would soon find for himself a nice warm spot on the mud bottom of the mill pond before Jack Frost touched the water with his icy fingers.

And Mr. John Hare had telephoned to the Old Red Rooster to come over and put up Mrs. Rabbit's storm-door and bank the cellar windows with dry leaves.

"Mother," said Little Jack Rabbit, as he polished the brass doorknob, "I guess Jack Frost will soon be around."

"Shouldn't wonder," she replied, "but who's afraid of Jack Frost? Danny Fox and Mr. Wicked Weasel, to say nothing of Hungry Hawk, are more to be feared." And that good lady rabbit began her ironing, for it was Tuesday, the day when all Rabbitville irons Monday's wash, I'm told.

Just then Bobbie Redvest began to sing:

The summer time is over,

And all the golden hours,

No more the roses crimson bloom

Amid the garden bowers.

The little birds have left their nests

And now are strong of wing,

They will not build themselves a home

Until the lovely spring,

But fly away to Southern lands,

Where warmth and sunshine reign,

They cannot brave the winter wind,

The snow drifts in the lane.

And little four-foot furry folks

Will safely hide away,

And sleep until the winter's past

And Spring has come to stay.

AN ACCIDENT

WELL, after Uncle John Hare had spent about a week at the Old Bramble Patch, he thought it time to go home. So he called up his house and ordered his Bunnymobile sent for him.

"Now don't worry about Little Jack Rabbit," he said to the anxious lady bunny, "I'll take good care of him and send him home safe and sound."

Then he put on his goggles while the little rabbit cranked up the Bunnymobile, and off they went.

You see, Uncle John was so fond of his little rabbit nephew that he just had to take him out for a drive.

But, goodness me. They had gone only a little way when they ran into a load of hay. And, oh dear me! It tumbled down on top of them and hid the Bunnymobile from sight. Wasn't that dreadful?

Well, I don't know what would have happened—they would have been smothered or had hay fever, I guess—if a big Circus Elephant hadn't come hurrying along just then.

Well, sir! He wound his trunk around that pile of hay and put it back on the wagon. Then he dropped in his pocket the nickel the farmer gave him, but he wouldn't take the carrot cent that grateful Uncle John offered him.

"I'm so nervous you'd better drive," cried the old gentleman hare. So Little Jack Rabbit took the wheel and for a little whileeverything went along nicely. But pretty soon it grew dark, so the little rabbit hopped out to light the lamps. But when he struck a match he found that the lamps were smashed to pieces. You see, they had hit the back of the hay wagon.

"What shall we do?"

"Get in and go along the best you can," answered the old gentleman hare. "We ought to be pretty near home by this time." And I guess they would have reached his little red house in a few minutes if the Policeman Dog hadn't stopped them.

"What do you mean by running your Bunnymobile without lights?" he growled. "I'll fine you ten bones!"

"Make it carrots and I'll pay you," said Uncle John.

But the Policeman Dog wouldn't take carrots. You see, he liked bones much better. Then he jumped on the running board and told them to drive to Station House No. 13.

But wasn't it lucky? They had gone only a little way when they came to a butcher shop, where Uncle John traded ten carrots for ten bones. And when he gave them to the Policeman dog, he told them they might drive home slowly.

But, oh dear me. All of a sudden a big owl gave a hooty toot. No sooner did the two little rabbits hear that dreadful noise than they hopped out of the Bunnymobile and into a hollow stump. "You'll be safe, now," said a little grasshopper from her Clover Patch House, nearby.

TWO PIGEONS

WELL, I'm going to tell you right away that the two little rabbits got safely home, although they had to hide all night in the hollow stump from the old owl. But the grasshopper stayed in the clover patch and built a little house with a front-door latch.

Well, as soon as they had run the Bunnymobile in the garage, they went into the little red house, and had breakfast. After that was over Little Jack Rabbit said good-by and hopped off home to the Old Bramble Patch. And while he was hopping along who should come by but old Professor Jim Crow with his little Black Book.

"Helloa there, little rabbit," said the wise old bird, and then he opened his little Black Book and, turning to page 23, he said:

"Let me read you something about pigeons."

"Why?" asked the little bunny, wiggling his little pink nose so fast that old Professor Jim Crow's eyes filled with tears, and he had to take off his spectacles and wipe them with his silk pocket handkerchief.

"Because," answered the old crow, "two pigeons have made their home in the loft of your mother's old barn." Then he put on his spectacles again and commenced to read aloud:

"Pigeons always lay two eggs, and these produce a male and a female, so they are mated from birth, and, could they remain so, they would be the happiest of winged beings."

And then the old professor closed his book and said, "Better hurry home and see the new pigeons." So away hopped the little rabbit, clipperty clip, lipperty lip, over the Sunny Meadow until, by and by, after awhile, he came to the Old Bramble Patch. There stood his mother in the backyard. She had just placed a pan of water under a tree for the pigeons.

"Don't make any noise," she said, as the little rabbit drew near. Pretty soon Mr. Pigeon flew down to taste the water, and by and by Mrs. Pigeon fluttered down by his side.

"Cock-a-doodle-do,

Of pigeons we have two,

But some day there'll be dozens more

A-cooing by the old barn door,"

sang the old Red Rooster who had come over from Uncle John's to help Mrs. Rabbit weed the carrot patch.

After that she and her little bunny boy hopped up on the front porch to hear the canary bird in her gold cage sing:

"I wouldn't be a pigeon

And live in an old red barn,

I'd rather be here when the weather is drear

And watch Mrs. Bunny darn."

Which made the kind lady rabbit laugh, for she spent lots of time, let me tell you, darning the holes in her little bunny boy's golf stockings.

MISS PUSSY

The pumpkins in the cornfield

Are as yellow as can be,

And the apples, red and golden,

Are hanging on the tree,

The grapes in purple clusters

Are swinging on the vine,

And the old crow's nest is empty

Upon the lonely pine.

"HA, ha," shouted Little Jack Rabbit, as Billy Breeze blew across the Sunny Meadow, and, let me tell you, Billy Breeze was just a little bit chilly, this cool November morning.

"I wonder what I'll do," thought the little rabbit, and he wiggled his little pink nose sideways, and then off he went, clipperty clip, lipperty lip, and by and by he came to an old hollow stump. So he peeked in, and then, all of a sudden, a purring voice asked:

"What are you doing, Mr. Curious One?"

"Oh, I wasn't doing anything wrong," answered the little bunny. "I just wanted to see what was inside."

"Well, I'll show you," answered the voice, and out popped a little black cat, with green eyes and a pink ribbon.

"Oh, it's you, Miss Pussy," laughed the little rabbit. "I'm glad it wasn't a bear or a wildcat," and he laughed some more and wiggled his little pink nose just for fun, you understand.

"What are you doing out here?"

"Looking for mice," answered the little black pussy.

"Don't you bother Timmy Meadowmouse," said Little Jack Rabbit quickly; "he's a friend of mine."

And then, what do you suppose happened? Why, the Farmer's dog came by, and away went the little rabbit, and up went Miss Pussy Cat's back, and her tail grew so big that had she tried to get back into the hollow stump I guess she would have had to leave her tail behind her! But she didn't. No sireemam. She just humped her back and meowed, and the Farmer's dog kept right on after Little Jack Rabbit, but of course he never caught him.

Well, as soon as the little bunny was safe in the Shady Forest, he looked about him, and pretty soon, not so very long, he saw Professor Jim Crow with his little Black Book under his wing.

"Read me something, won't you please," begged the little rabbit. So the old professor bird took out his book and turned over the pages until he came to "The early worm must look out for the bird."

"Ha, ha," laughed the little rabbit. "I must tell that to mother. She always tells it the other way 'round." Then off he hopped, and the old black bird flew away to his tree in Kalamazoo. For that was the name of the little village where Professor Crow has his home, and where he taught in the grammar school arithmetic and the Golden Rule, and sometimes Latin and sometimes Greek, and anything else that a bird can speak. Goodness me, if my typewriter hasn't made up this poetry all by itself. I wonder where it went to school.

A BUSY BEAVER

"BUNNY BOY!" called Little Jack Rabbit's mother, oh, so early, as Mr. Merry Sun climbed up the blue gray sky of the early morning, "Get up, little bunny!"

So the little rabbit hopped out of bed; and after he had combed his hair with a little chip, he ran downstairs to ask his mother about the early worm Professor Jim Crow had mentioned in the last story. After breakfast he hopped out on the Sunny Meadow and looked about him. Mr. Merry Sun was shining down on the frosty dew and Billy Breeze was very chilly, and the meadow grass brown and withered. It didn't look at all like the lovely Sunny Meadow.

"Oh, dear," sighed the little rabbit, "all the flowers are gone, and most of the birds have flown to the sunny South." Just then Professor Jim Crow flew by with his little Black Book under his wing:

"Helloa, there, little bunny, how are you this chilly day?" And then that old crow began to read out of his little book:

"Little rabbit's coat of brown

Soon will turn to white.

Then among the snowy drifts

He can hide from sight.

"You see how Mother Nature looks after you," said that wise old blackbird. "In the summer your coat is brown like the dry grass and brambles. But when winter comes it turns white so that you won't be seen so well against the snow."

Then away flew Professor Jim Crow to read his little Black Book to somebody else, and the little rabbit hopped along and by and by he came to the Bubbling Brook where the speckled trout swam in and out among the rocks and the little fresh water crabs played in the quiet pools. All of a sudden down fell a tree.

"There," said Busy Beaver, "I'll now have some logs to make a dam."

"Why do you want a dam? Do you want to spoil the Bubbling Brook?"

"It won't spoil the brook," answered the little beaver. "It will only make it deep so that when I build my house for the winter my front door won't freeze up tight."

"Oh, I see," said Little Jack Rabbit, and he wiggled his little pink nose sideways. "And how soon will you have it finished?"

"Oh, long before Old Mr. North Wind brings the snow," answered Busy Beaver.

Old Mr. North Wind

On his Snow Horse,

Swiftly is riding

Down the golf course,

Over the meadow

And up the steep hill,

Shouting so hoarsely;

"Gid ap, there, Bill!"

DON'T WORRY

IN the last story Little Jack Rabbit, of Old Bramble Patch, U. S. A., was talking to Busy Beaver, who was making a dam across the Bubbling Brook, you remember, to keep the water from freezing up his front door in the cold winter time.

"Every one is getting ready for the cold weather. It won't be long before my dam is finished and then I'll set to work and make my house of mud and sticks," and Busy Beaver jumped into the water with a flap of his broad tail and disappeared. So the little rabbit hopped along, and by and by he came to the cave where the Big Brown Bear made his home.

"Helloa!" said Little Jack Rabbit, as the Big Brown Bear looked out of his front door. "Winter time will soon be here."

"Oh, that doesn't worry me," said the Big Brown Bear.

"But what will you eat?" asked the little rabbit.

"When you're asleep you don't feel hungry. On a warm sunny day I may come out for a little while and find something to eat. I don't worry."

Worry never makes you fat,

Instead, it makes you lean.

Never worry for a minute, —

Worry has the devil in it, —

Keep your mind serene.

And if you don't know what "serene" means, take your father's dictionary and look up, for the more words you know the wiser you'll grow.

"Well, I don't have to worry about the cold weather," laughed the little rabbit. "Mother Nature will give me a new white fur overcoat, and the Old Bramble Patch will keep the wind away, and the cabbage leaves which mother and I have stored away will last all winter." And then away he went to see more of his friends in the Shady Forest.

Well, by and by, after a while, he heard the honk of an automobile horn. "I wonder whether that's Uncle John," and Little Jack Rabbit stopped and looked all around, and pretty soon, not very long, Mr. John Hare drove by in his Bunnymobile. He looked very fine in his polkadot handkerchief and gold watch and chain and a great big immense diamond horseshoe pin in his pink cravat. Oh, my, yes! Uncle John was quite a dandy. He was the best dressed Hare in Harebridge, and why shouldn't he be when you consider he was President of the bank and the Harum Scarum Club!

"Helloa, there, little nephew," he shouted.

"Hop in and take a ride with me,

We'll take a spin for a mile or three,

And maybe we'll come where the lollypops grow,

Pink and yellow, all in a row."

THE LITTLE FROSTY PAINTER

There's a little frosty painter

Who soon will come around

To put a silver edging on

The grasses on the ground,

Upon the window pane he'll paint

A fairy landscape, strange and quaint,

And some cold morning you'll awake

To find he's frosted Mother's cake.

NOW can you guess who this little frosty painter is? Why, it's Jack Frost, the son of King Winter.

"Ha, ha," crowed the Weathercock on the Big Red Barn. "Jack Frost is here, for I can see the silver frost upon the grass in the Sunny Meadow," and then that gilded rooster turned his head to the North and blew on his gilt toes to keep them warm.

Pretty soon Old Sic'em walked out of his little dog house and shook himself. "Bow wow," he said, "it's a chilly morning."

"Cock-a-doodle-do," said Cocky Doodle, and then Henny Penny cackled loudly:

"I've laid an egg so white and clean

'Twould grace a breakfast for a queen.

But if a little girl should beg

The farmer for my pretty egg,

I'd tell him quick to let her go

And take my egg as white as snow."

As the little hen finished her song, she noticed Little Jack Rabbit by the Old Rail Fence.

"Helloa, Mrs. Henny Penny," he said. "I like your song. If I see any poor little girl I'll tell her!" and then the little rabbit hopped away, for he just couldn't stay a moment in one place, let me tell you. He wanted to be on the hop, skip and jump all the time, just like lots of little boys and girls I know.

Well, by and by, after a while, he saw Old Professor Jim Crow scratching his head with his claw.

"What's the matter?" asked the little rabbit.

"I can't make out something I've written in my little Black Book," answered the old black bird, and he scratched his head again and looked dreadfully perplexed, which means worse than worried, you know.

"Let me look," said Little Jack Rabbit. And when the old blackbird had flown down from his pine tree, the little bunny leaned over his shoulder, and read: "Oh, oh, oh, Squirreltown!"

"Why, that's the Squirrel Brothers telephone number," he laughed. "So it is," said Professor Jim Crow. "I'm so glad you told me! Let's call them up!"

"'One, three, five, Chestnut Hill!'

Keep on ringing, Central, till

Some one answers, 'Hello! who

Is calling up my Bungaloo!'

"But if no one says a word;

Not a twitter from a bird,

Nor a chatter comes your way,

Call again another day."

GRANDPA POSSUM

BUT! gracious me! Central gave Little Jack Rabbit the wrong number, for as he stood in the Hollow Stump Telephone Booth, with the receiver to his ear, he heard Grandpa Possum say:

"I don't care how hard it snows,

Nor how Old Mr. North Wind blows,

For I'm as safe as safe can be

In a big warm hole in the old nut tree."

"Ha, ha!" laughed the little rabbit, hopping out of the booth, just as Grandpa Possum poked his head out of his hollow tree house, "you certainly look sleepy. What made you wake up?"

"What woke me?" asked the possum gentleman angrily. "Why, those good for nothing Squirrel Brothers threw a snowball into my window." And then Grandpa Possum shook the snow out of his left ear and looked around to find those naughty squirrels.

All of a sudden, quicker than a wink, another snowball hit the old hollow tree a tre-men-dous whack.

"Goodness me!" said Grandpa Possum, "if I ever catch those pesky squirrels I'll make them wince, yes, I will, as sure as I'm twenty-one!"

And he began to grin, for Grandpa Possum is full of good nature and never can stay angry very long.

"If you're good natured, every one

Will love you more and more,

So don't get mad, be always glad,

And lend a helping paw,"

sang Grandpa Possum, winking at Little Jack Rabbit, as Squirrel Twinkle Tail peeked out and said:

"Excuse me, Grandpa Possum,

For throwing snow at you,

'Twould be too bad to make you mad

Or just a little blue."

And then he and his mischievous brother Featherhead ran away and didn't bother Grandpa Possum for a long time.

"Well, I guess I'll be getting along," said the little rabbit and he hopped away and by and by he came to the Shady Forest Pond where Busy Beaver had his home. But of course he wasn't anywhere to be seen. No, siree. He was in his little mud hut whose roof stuck up above the ice and whose cellar door was way down deep where the water was free from ice and he could swim in and out as he pleased.

So the little rabbit didn't wait, but hopped along until he came to the edge of the forest, when he started to hop across the Sunny Meadow to the Old Barn Yard where Henny Penny and Cocky Doodle lived all the year 'round. But just then he heard the supper bell. So, instead, he hurried home to be in time for Aunt Jemima's angel cake.

COUSIN CHATTERBOX

LITTLE JACK RABBIT loved the snow that covered the ground with a soft white carpet. His feet never grew cold. No siree, they didn't. All the little Forest Folk liked the snow, for Loving Mother Nature had given them warm fur, and warm fur laughs at cold just as love laughs at troubles.

Even Mrs. Grouse was happy. And if you've forgotten why, I'll tell you again. It was because dear Mother Nature had given her a pair of snow-shoes. Yes, indeed. The skin had grown out between her toes until she could walk as nicely as you please over the snow. And what is more, Loving Mother Nature had taught her to dive into a snowbank where she could stay for the night as snug and warm as you please, when Old Mr. North Wind blew upon his chilly horn.

Neither did Squirrel Nutcracker care that the ground was covered with snow, and he could find no more nuts. He had a supply hidden safely away in the old hollow chestnut tree. But he did mind having other people take them. And when his cousin, Chatterbox, in his red fur coat, tried to break into his storehouse, Squirrel Nutcracker was as mad as mad could be.

"Whoever steals a nut from me

From out my storehouse in this tree,

A friend of mine shall be no more,

So let him stay outside my store."

Chatterbox grew very angry as he peeped down from the chestnut tree and saw Little Jack Rabbit with a big smile on his face. It told the naughty red squirrel that the little rabbit knew whom the little gray squirrel meant.

But when Little Jack Rabbit opened his knapsack and took out a lemon lollypop, you should have seen those two squirrels forget all about their quarrel and scramble down the big chestnut tree. Yes, sir. Squirrel Nutcracker forgot that Chatterbox wanted to steal his nuts, and Chatterbox forgot that he had been caught! And now that I come to think it over, perhaps that is the reason the little bunny laughed just before he opened his knapsack! I guess he knew how quickly those two little squirrels would forget everything when they saw a lemon lollypop!

"Now promise me one thing to-day,

You little squirrels, red and gray,

That you will quarrel nevermore

Nor steal a nut from any store.

For he who steals will always end

In having neither love nor friend."

Now don't you think it wonderful that the little rabbit could make up such lovely poetry? Well, I do, but the two little squirrels thought what he does in the next story even more wonderful.

But you must not impatient get,

If mother says, it's growing late.

Just wait until another time,

And kiss good-night your Auntie Kate.

JIMMY JAY

NOW just as I finished the last story Little Jack Rabbit handed Squirrel Nutcracker and Chatterbox each a lovely lemon lollypop. I would have told you that before, only I had no more room, so I had to wait. But it's a good thing the little Squirrels didn't have to wait, isn't it?

Well, after the lemon lollypops were all gone, the little bunny went upon his way, hipperty hop, lipperty lop, until he saw Jimmy Jay on the Old Rail Fence.

Now you know that Jimmy Jay is a very mischievous little bird. Yes, sir, he certainly loves to tease. Grandmother Magpie is mischievous, too, but she's no worse than little Jimmy Jay. She does harm by meddling and Jimmy Jay by teasing.

Yes, it certainly is too bad that such a pretty bird as Jimmy Jay should cause so much trouble. Why, his coat's as blue as the summer sky when Mr. Merry Sun is shining at his best.

"Hip, hip, hurray,

I'm Jimmy Jay,

And I'm proud of my coat of blue.

Go on your way,

I'm Jimmy Jay,

I've no time to talk to you."

"You're too fond of yourself, Jimmy Jay," said Little Jack Rabbit, and he wiggled his pink nose till the little Jay bird almost fell off the rail. You see, Little Jack Rabbit had the habit of wiggling his nose so fast that it made everybody dizzy to look at it.

"Mother says it's not the clothes

You wear that make you good;

It's having a contented mind

And doing what you should."

Then away hopped the little rabbit, leaving Jimmy Jay to think it over. Perhaps it kept that mischievous little Jay Bird from looking at himself in the Bubbling Brook. Or maybe it was because it was all frozen over with a thick coat of ice.

Well, anyway, the little rabbit hopped along for maybe a mile or maybe less, until he came to a little hole in snow, when, all of a sudden, out popped Timmy Meadowmouse. You see in the winter time, Timmy Meadowmouse makes little tunnels under the snow, and every once in a while, here and there, he climbs up a stiff stalk of grass and pokes out his head to look around. And wasn't he glad to see the little rabbit. Well, I just guess he was. But if he had seen Danny Fox instead he wouldn't have been so pleased. No sireemam. And in the next story, if the little meadowmouse doesn't play hide-and-seek in the snow till that sly old fox comes around, I'll tell you what happened after this.

THE TIP OF A TAIL

NOW let us see—oh, yes, I remember now. We left off just when little Timmy Meadowmouse poked his head up through the snow and said, "Helloa!"

"Howdy, Timmy Meadowmouse,

Through the chimney of your house

Looking o'er the meadow white,

Glancing round from left to right,

You might lose your woollen socks

If 't weren't I, but Danny Fox,"

laughed Little Jack Rabbit, kicking up his strong hind legs until a big snowball hit Timmy Meadowmouse, knocking the hat off his head into a snowbank.

"Look out! What are you doing," cried Timmy Meadowmouse. "That's the new hat Mother gave me for Xmas." Pretty soon he began to laugh, too, for he's a merry little fellow and a good friend.

"My, but it's lonely these long winter days," sighed the little bunny. "Everybody's sound asleep in his winter home. Only you and I and a few others are about," and the little rabbit sighed again, for what he says is true, let me tell you.

For in the good Old Summer time

'Most everybody's round,

The feathered folk are in the trees,

The furry on the ground.

And all the sweet and verdant dells

Are ringing with the flower bells.

"Cheer up, little rabbit," said the merry little Meadowmouse, "spring will soon be here. The buds on the trees are waiting for little Miss South Wind to open them," and after that the little meadowmouse disappeared into his tunnel and the little bunny hopped away, clipperty clip, over the snow till he came to the Shady Forest. And after he had gone in a little way, not so very far, he saw something that made his heart go pitter, pat. And what do you suppose it was? I'll give you three guesses and then I'll tell you. The footprints of Danny Fox. Yes, sir! Right there in the snow were the marks of that sly old fox's feet.

Little Jack Rabbit stopped right then and there to look about him. But Danny Fox was nowhere in sight, but that was no reason why he might not be, at that very moment, hiding behind a tree. The little rabbit looked again at the footprints in the snow. There they were, but, thank goodness! They led away, far away, into the Shady Forest. Just then, all of a sudden, the Miller's Boy jumped out from behind a clump of bushes.

"Run! run!" screamed Jimmy Jay, who happened by just then. And the little rabbit did. He went so fast that his shadow couldn't keep up with him and neither could the Miller's Boy. But, oh, dear me! The Miller's dog did. Yes, sir! He kept so close that before he popped into the Old Bramble Patch he caught the end of the little rabbit's tail.

OLD BARNEY OWL

WELL, I'm mighty glad the little rabbit lost only the fur tip to his tail. That was bad enough, but he forgot all about it the next morning when the Squirrel Brothers invited him over the 'phone to meet them at the Shady Forest Pond. He spent no time at all getting out his skates, but his mother took two minutes and a half tying a woolen muffler around his neck. She knew, like all wise mothers, that it's lots more fun to skate when one is nice and warm.

When he reached the pond the Squirrel Brothers were already there, skating merrily over the ice.

Busy Beaver in his winter home below could hear them whirring along, cutting fancy figures in the ice, and calling merrily to one another.

After a while, when the little rabbit and the squirrel brothers had grown tired of skating, they ran over to make a call on Old Barney Owl, who lived in the Big Chestnut Tree on a small island, right in the middle of the pond.

Although it was now pretty late in the afternoon, the old gentleman owl was still asleep, and when he opened the door, his eyes winked and blinked, and at first he didn't know them at all. In fact, he shut the door right in their faces. I suppose he thought they had knocked just to wake him up. Perhaps they had, for when the door closed with a bang they all began to laugh.

By and by Featherhead knocked again, and when Old Barney Owl opened it a second time, the naughty little squirrel said:

"Here is a nice fresh egg!"

Goodness me! When the old owl, whose eyes were still very blinky, found out it wasn't an egg, but a snowball, he dropped it on the little squirrel's head, and slammed the door again.

Now, if Featherhead had only gone back to his skating, all would have been well. But he didn't. No, indeed. Instead, he knocked again, and when the old owl opened the door, that naughty squirrel dropped a snowball down his collar. Goodness gracious me! What a scuffle there was all at

once, and, just like that! the old owl pulled the little squirrel into his house
and closed the door.

Oh, what a scowl had Mr. Owl,

And Featherhead felt nearly dead.

He was so scared at what he'd done

He couldn't move his feet to run.

And, goodness gracious! so would I

Have felt as if I'd surely die,

If some big giant from his tree

Had through his doorway pulled poor me.

From head to toe I'd surely quake,

And feel my frightened heart would break.

But now let's turn the page to see

If ever Featherhead gets free.

"HELP! HELP!"

LITTLE JACK RABBIT threw himself against the door as soon as it closed on Featherhead. But Old Barney Owl had fastened the latch and it wouldn't open. My! What a dreadful scuffling was going on inside.

"Open the door! Open the door!" shouted the little rabbit, pounding on the wooden panels with his strong hind feet. But Old Barney Owl paid no attention. Maybe he had all he could do to hold Featherhead.

By and by it grew very quiet and Twinkle Tail peeped in through the keyhole, but he couldn't see anything.

"Oh, dear me!" cried Little Jack Rabbit. "Perhaps Old Barney Owl has eaten Featherhead!" Poor Twinkle Tail's heart almost stopped beating. Maybe it would have if he had known that the old owl had dragged his little brother squirrel upstairs by the tail.

"Snowballs and eggs! Snowballs and eggs!" muttered Old Barney, shaking Featherhead until his teeth rattled. "You little rascal! You thought I couldn't tell a snowball from an egg, eh?" and he gave the little squirrel another shake.

"Now I'm going to skin you and eat you for supper!"

Oh, dear me! How Featherhead trembled when he heard that.

Just then there came a tremendous crash downstairs, and as the old owl looked over the railing, Twinkle Tail and Little Jack Rabbit broke in the door.

"Help! Help!" shouted Featherhead.

"Rats and mice! Rats and mice!" cried Old Barney Owl, still keeping a tight hold on the little squirrel's tail.

He knew there was going to be trouble, but he wasn't going to let his supper get away from him without a fight, let me tell you. No, siree. Old Barney Owl was too hungry for that. But he changed his mind pretty quickly. Yes, siree. When Little Jack Rabbit let fly his hind feet, thumpty-thump, thumpty-thump! knocking the old owl head over heels, he changed his mind. He let go of Featherhead, and before he could change it again there was nobody in the house except himself.

Gracious me! How the Squirrel Brothers scurried home. And the little rabbit lost no time, either. He went to bed early and in the middle of the night, when Old Barney Owl went "Hooty, toot!" he shivered and pulled the bedclothes up over his head.

"Toot, toot, hoot!"

Old Barney plays his flute.

It sounds so shivery in the dark,

The firefly's tiny gleaming spark,

Goes out because the firefly

Is frightened by the old owl's cry.

PUMPKIN PLACE P. O.

"LITTLE JACK RABBIT!" said his mother, the next morning, "run down to the postoffice and see if there's a letter for me." So the little rabbit put on his khaki cap and his little knapsack and started off, and by and by, after a while, he came to Rabbitville, where the postoffice stood on the corner of Pumpkin Place and Corn Cob Lane.

"Is there a letter for Mrs. John Rabbit, Old Bramble Patch, Rail Fence Corner, U. S. A.?" he asked the lady postmistress, an old maid grasshopper who worked for Uncle Sam in the winter and in the summer played in the wheat field.

"I think there is," she said, looking in box 13, and, sure enough, there was. Then she handed the letter to the little rabbit, and shut the door of the little window and after that she took out her vanity bag and powdered her nose.

The little rabbit put the letter in his knapsack and started home, but just as he reached the Shady Forest, whom should he see but Squirrel Nutcracker. The old gray squirrel had come out of his hollow tree for a little run in the sun. You see, on cold days he curled himself up in a ball and kept very quiet, but on warm days he came out and jumped from limb to limb to get the cramps out of his leg muscles.

"Where are you going, little rabbit?" he asked, and then he took a nut out of his pocket and cracked it with his sharp teeth without a bit of trouble.

"I've got a letter for mother," said Little Jack Rabbit, "and I mustn't stop to talk to any one," and he hopped along as fast as he could, for he was afraid he might lose the letter, you see. Well, pretty soon, not so very long, he came to the Old Bramble Patch, and after he had given the letter to his mother he hopped out on the Sunny Meadow, and just then, all of a sudden, Old Professor Jim Crow flew by. He had his little Black Book under his wing, and as soon as he saw the little rabbit he lighted on a bush and turned to page 23.

"Let me read you something," he said, putting on his spectacles, and after he had cawed three times and a half he began:

"Little rabbits should take care

To every morning comb their hair.

They always should be clean and neat

And keep their dispositions sweet."

And then that wise old bird looked up over his spectacles and winked at the little rabbit. "Did you comb your hair this morning?" he asked. And wasn't it lucky that Little Jack Rabbit hadn't forgotten to? Well, I just guess it was.

AN ICE CREAM PINE CONE

PRETTY soon it began to snow and soon the Sunny Meadow was just as white and smooth as Mrs. Rabbit's best table cloth, for the feathery snowflakes fell so softly you could almost hear the stillness. Little Jack Rabbit opened his knapsack and pulled out his rubber boots. Then he put on his ear muffs and his nice warm mittens and slung his knapsack over his back, but very carefully, for there were lots of nice things to eat in that knapsack. Yes, siree. His kind mother always filled it up with cakes and sweets. I guess the little rabbit knew that very morning his dear mother had baked lettuce cakes, and how he did love lettuce cakes. Yes, indeed he did, and so would you and so would I if we could only get one, I'm sure.

Well, after he had hopped along a little way, he began to sing,

"Three little bunnies a-sliding went

On a winter's day,

The ice was thin, and two fell in,

And the third one ran away."

"Ha, ha!" cawed an old crow from a tree top, "that's a very fine song!"

"Well, if you think it's such a fine song, throw me down an ice cream pine cone," said the little rabbit. But the selfish old crow wanted it for himself, and instead threw down a snowball, which hit the little rabbit on the tip of his tail.

The little rabbit wasn't going to stay there and have snowballs thrown at him. No, sireemam, he wasn't. And pretty soon, not so very far, he met Jimmy Mink creeping along by the Old Duck Pond.

"I have to be very careful these winter days," said the little mink. "Everybody wants to wear fur in the winter time, you know, and if that dreadful Miller's Boy sees me, he might shoot me and sell my fur for a muff!"

"They set traps for me," answered the little rabbit. "And Danny Fox and Mr. Wicked Weasel are always after me. And Hungry Hawk, too. You're not the only one who has to look out for himself."

Then the little rabbit took a lovely lollypop out of his knapsack and gave it to Jimmy Mink, and asked him to make a visit at the Old Bramble Patch.

"I'll get Uncle John to take us riding in his Bunnysnowbile." This tickled the little mink almost to pieces, for he'd never ridden in a Bunnysnowbile, and neither have I and neither have you, but perhaps some day we will if we happen to be around when Mr. John Hare comes by. And in the next book, if the smoke doesn't blow down our chimney and choke the cook so that she can't bake the biscuits for breakfast, I'll tell you more about Little Jack Rabbit and his friends who live in Bunnyville, U. S. A.

THE END